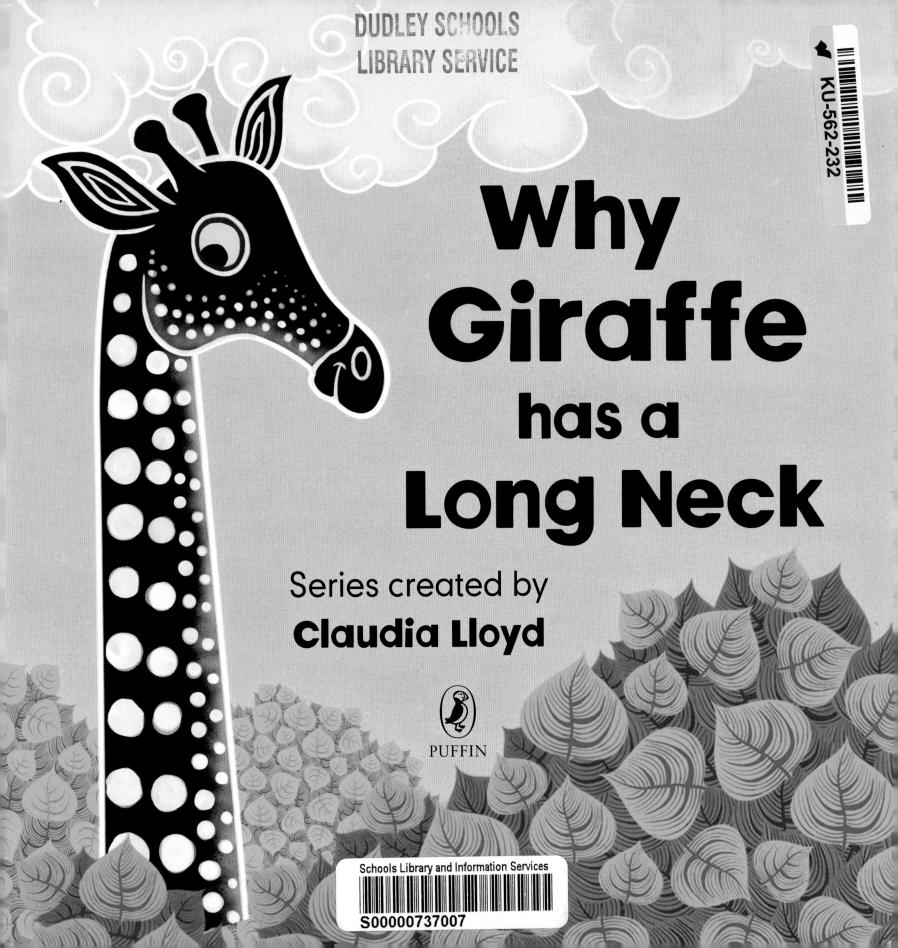

Why Giraffe has a Long Neck

Series created by

Claudia Lloyd

PUFFIN

Text based on the script written by Edward Gakuya and Claudia Lloyd.

Illustrations from the TV animation produced by Tiger Aspect Productions Limited and Homeboyz Entertainment Kenya.

Artwork supplied by Noah Mukono.

PUFFIN BOOKS:
Published by the Penguin Group: London, New York, Australia, Canada, India, Ireland, New Zealand and South Africa. Penguin Books Ltd, Registered Offices: 80 Strand, London WC2R 0RL, England. Published in Puffin Books 2011.

Made and printed in China.

001 – 10 9 8 7 6 5 4 3 2 1

ISBN: 978-0-141-33505-6

"**Jambo, Giraffe.**
Have a mango.
They're **mangolicious!**"

You see there was a time

when Giraffe had **short** legs, **short** horns and a very

short, **stumpy** neck. She was also a very **fussy eater.**

"What's the **problem**, Giraffe?"
asked Tickbird.

"I've got a **runny tummy.**
Too many mangoes,
I think," said Giraffe.

The other animals tried to help.
"Why don't you try eating
some **lettuce?**" said Tortoise.

"Eat some **grass**," said Hippo.
"It does wonders for an
upset tummy."

"**Honey**, that's what you need,"
said Lion. "Go straight to
the bees and ask them for
some honey."

"**Honey!**
I'll go straight to the
bees and get
some honey.

Asante! Thank you, everyone."

On the way to the bees, Giraffe met Chameleon.

"Hi, Giraffe, **jambo.**
Why the sad face?"

"Well, I've got a spot
of **tummy trouble**
and Lion thought a bit of honey
might make it go away."

"The honey's inside the tree," buzzed the bees. "**Help yourself.** Hope you feel better."

The bees buzzed off.

"**Wow! Free honey!**
What are you waiting for?
Push your head inside that
hole and get that honey
right now!"

So Giraffe pushed her head inside
the tree and found lots of . . .

"Chameleon, is my tummy **rumbling?**"
called Giraffe from the inside of the tree.

"**No tummy rumbles** to report!" shouted Chameleon.

"I can't get my head **out** of this tree," called Giraffe. "But don't worry – I'll be all right because there's **lots** of yummy honey in here."

"But you can't **stay** in there, Giraffe!" said Chameleon. "I'm going for **help.**"

Night-time came and
Giraffe **slurped**
and **slurped.**

"slurp,

slurp . . ."

Then morning came, and Giraffe **slurped** and **slurped.**

"You see what I'm saying?" said Chameleon. "Giraffe is **stuck** inside the tree."

"slurp slurp . . ."

"May I make a suggestion, Your Majesty?" said Tortoise. "May I suggest we pull Giraffe out by her **legs!**"

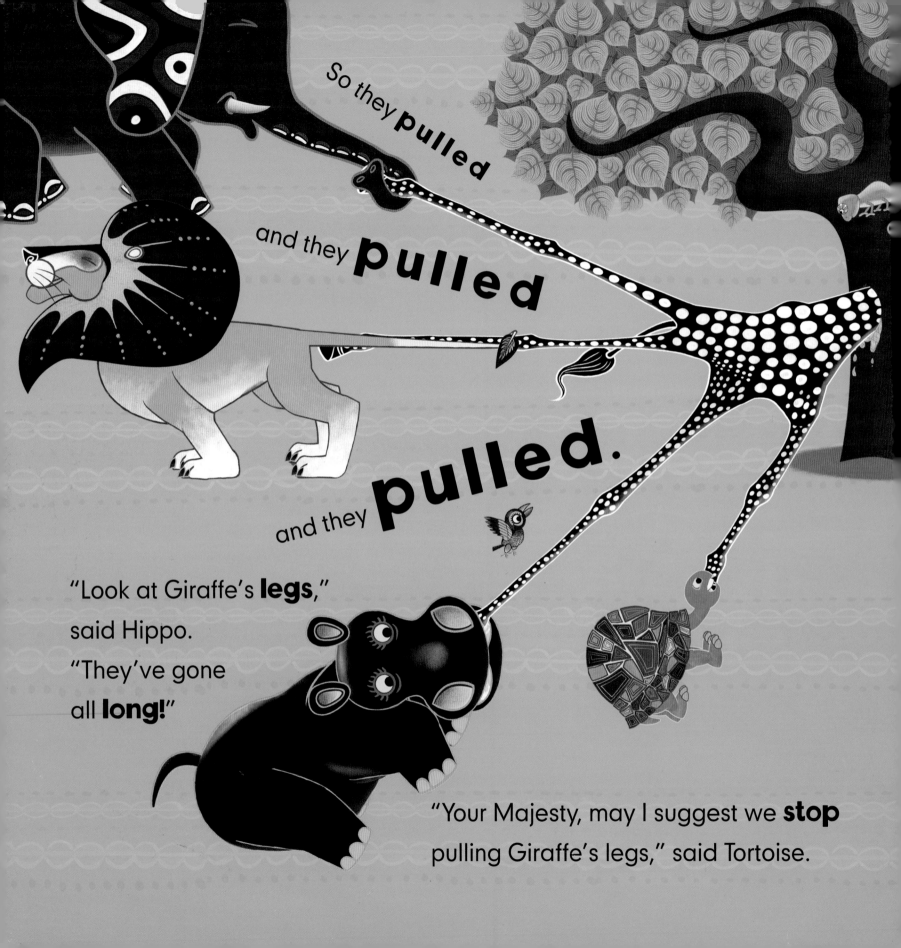

So they **pulled**

and they **pulled**

and they **pulled.**

"Look at Giraffe's **legs**,"
said Hippo.
"They've gone
all **long!**"

"Your Majesty, may I suggest we **stop**
pulling Giraffe's legs," said Tortoise.

"Don't worry, Giraffe," shouted Lion.

"We **will** get you out of there."

"Well, it looks like you and me will be here for **quite some time**," said Chameleon. "I know, let's play **I went into the jungle.**

I went into the jungle and I found . . . a **mango.**"

"Oh, I love this game," said Giraffe. "**I went into the jungle** and I found a **mango . . .**

and a **big yellow stone.**"

"**I went into the jungle**
and I found a **mango**,
a **big yellow stone** and a
. . . **spotty caterpillar.**"

"**I went into the jungle**
and I found a **mango**,
a **big yellow stone**,
a **spotty caterpillar**,
and . . . some **nuts.**"

And while they were playing,
Giraffe's tree grew taller,
the leaves turned brown
and **autumn** came!

The animals wondered
what to do.

"... an ostrich **egg** ... a **coconut** ... a flamingo **feather** ..."

Then Monkey had an idea.
"I know, let's **pull** the tree **off** Giraffe!"

"**Why not?**" said Tortoise.
"We haven't got
another plan."

So they **pulled** and they **pulled**

and they **pulled** until . . .

"**Stop!**
Stop!
Stop!

Giraffe's **neck** is
s t r e t c h i n g !"

"Don't you worry!" called Lion.
"We **will** get you out, Giraffe."

"Here we go **again**,"
sighed Chameleon.

"I went into the jungle and I found . . ."

And while they were playing,
Giraffe's tree grew **even** taller, all its leaves
dropped off and **winter** came!

"...an **orange**...a **mushroom**..."

"Giraffe, are you **all right?**"
asked Tickbird.

"Oh, I'm **fine**. Chameleon's been
keeping me company and we've
been having a **lovely** time."

They kept on playing and Giraffe's tree grew **even taller**, new leaves appeared and **spring** came!

"... an empty **seed pod** ... a **prickly pear** ..."

"Oh my **goodness**, look how **long** Giraffe's **neck** is now!" said Tortoise.

"Giraffe, are you all right in there?"

"Well, actually I'm getting a little bit bored now and I've run out of **honey!**"

"Giraffe," said Chameleon, "you've **got** to try **pulling** yourself out **one more** time."

"Do you think I **could** do it?" asked Giraffe.

"Well, you have changed quite a bit," replied Chameleon.

"OK," said Giraffe. "Here I **go . . .**"

And **tall**, **thin** Giraffe pulled herself out of the tree!

POP!

"I'm **out**, I'm **out**! I'm **free**...

Oh! You're all such a **long way** away!"

"That's because you're so **tall**," called Hippo from down below.

"Well, I'm not sure I have a head for **heights**," said Giraffe. "How long have I been up here?"

"Three whole **seasons** and the height of this **tree!**" replied Chameleon.

And with her new long **neck**, Giraffe found her very own **food** right at the top of the trees that no other animal could reach.

"Mmmm, yummy fresh new leaves. **Delicious!**"

"And no more **tummy** trouble!"

So **that's why**
Giraffe has a long neck.
She **stretched** and **stretched**
inside the tree, and now
her head almost touches
the **clouds!**